My mom got me to stop by having me wear this mitten to bed.

I was never a thumb sucker, but I chewed my pinky. Actually, I still do.

I sucked my thumb till I was thirteen.

My name is _____. I stopped sucking my thumb when I was _____ years old.

THUMB
LOVE

Elise Primavera

robin corey books
New York

All rights reserved. Published in the United States by Robin Corey Books, an imprint of Random House Children's Books,
a division of Random House, Inc., 1745 Broadway, New York, NY 10019.

Robin Corey Books and the colophon are trademarks of Random House, Inc.

Visit us on the Web! www.randomhouse.com/kids
www.robincoreybooks.com

Educators and librarians, for a variety of teaching tools, visit us at www.randomhouse.com/teachers

Library of Congress Cataloging-in-Publication Data
Primavera, Elise.
Thumb love / by Elise Primavera.—1st ed.
p. cm.
Summary: Unable to kick her thumb-sucking habit, Lulu develops a twelve-step program to help.
ISBN 978-0-375-84481-2 (hardcover) — ISBN 978-0-375-95182-4 (Gibraltar lib. bdg.)
[1. Thumb sucking—Fiction. 2. Humorous stories.] I. Title.
PZ7.P9354Thu 2010
[E]—dc22   2009042265

MANUFACTURED IN MALAYSIA

10 9 8 7 6 5 4 3 2 1

First Edition

Hello. My name is Lulu and I'm a thumb sucker.
Hello, Lulu.
Hi.
Hi, Lulu.

Lulu and her Thumb were very happy together. In sickness and in health, in good times and in bad, Lulu and her Thumb were best friends.

The Thumb was great to have on a busy day and kept her busy on a lazy day.

In fact, Lulu didn't know what she would do without her wonderful, beautiful Thumb.

"I love you," Lulu told her Thumb.

"Ditto," the Thumb told Lulu.

The Thumb was always fun at the beach,

in the park,

watching TV,

with a book,

by a brook,

on Mondays, Tuesdays, *any* day.

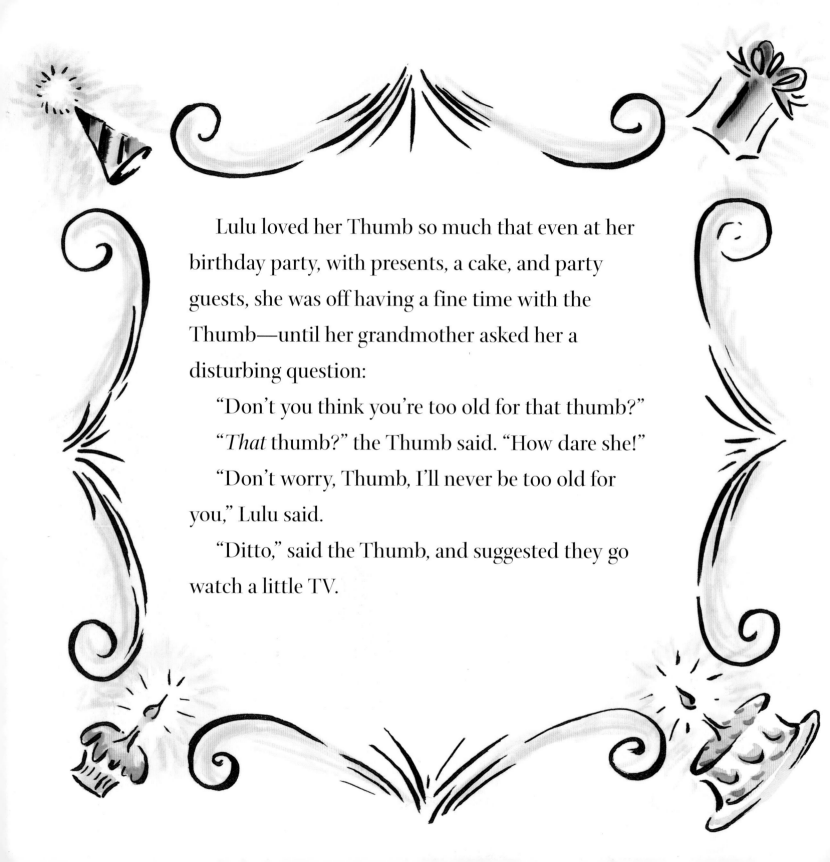

Lulu loved her Thumb so much that even at her birthday party, with presents, a cake, and party guests, she was off having a fine time with the Thumb—until her grandmother asked her a disturbing question:

"Don't you think you're too old for that thumb?"

"*That* thumb?" the Thumb said. "How dare she!"

"Don't worry, Thumb, I'll never be too old for you," Lulu said.

"Ditto," said the Thumb, and suggested they go watch a little TV.

Nestled into her favorite chair, surrounded by the
soft glow of the TV set, Lulu snuggled up with her
fuzzy blue blanket and the Thumb.

"Comfy?" asked the Thumb.

"Very," Lulu sighed.

Everything was perfect—except for the snickering.

That's right, *snickering*—right at Lulu and her Thumb.

"Some people just don't know what's good," Lulu grumbled.

"You are SO right!" the Thumb agreed.

The next day Lulu and the Thumb went to the
beach with her family. But later that afternoon gray
clouds rolled in, and Lulu and her Thumb wanted to
leave. As the sky darkened, Lulu's mother said, "That
thumb is going to make your teeth stick out someday."

"No it won't," Lulu said. "Maybe some thumbs—but not *my* Thumb."

"Baby!" someone yelled.

Lulu just frowned and thought about sleeping over with her favorite cousin Lili, who loved *her* thumb, too.

Later that night Lulu thought she heard—no, it couldn't be, but it sounded like— "Are you still doing that?"

"What?" said Lulu.

"Sucking your *thumb*?!" Lili replied. "I stopped doing *that* ages ago!"

"You're going to be sorry," said Lili, "if you keep sucking that thumb. It's going to push your teeth straight out and your tongue straight forward, *and* they say it will affect your speech."

"*Who* says?" Lulu cried.

"Thumb Experts, that's who!" Lili rolled over and went to sleep.

Lulu felt sad and alone.

"Don't listen to her," whispered the Thumb. "Come on, kid, it's you and me against the world, right?"

"Right," said Lulu, and soon she fell asleep, too.

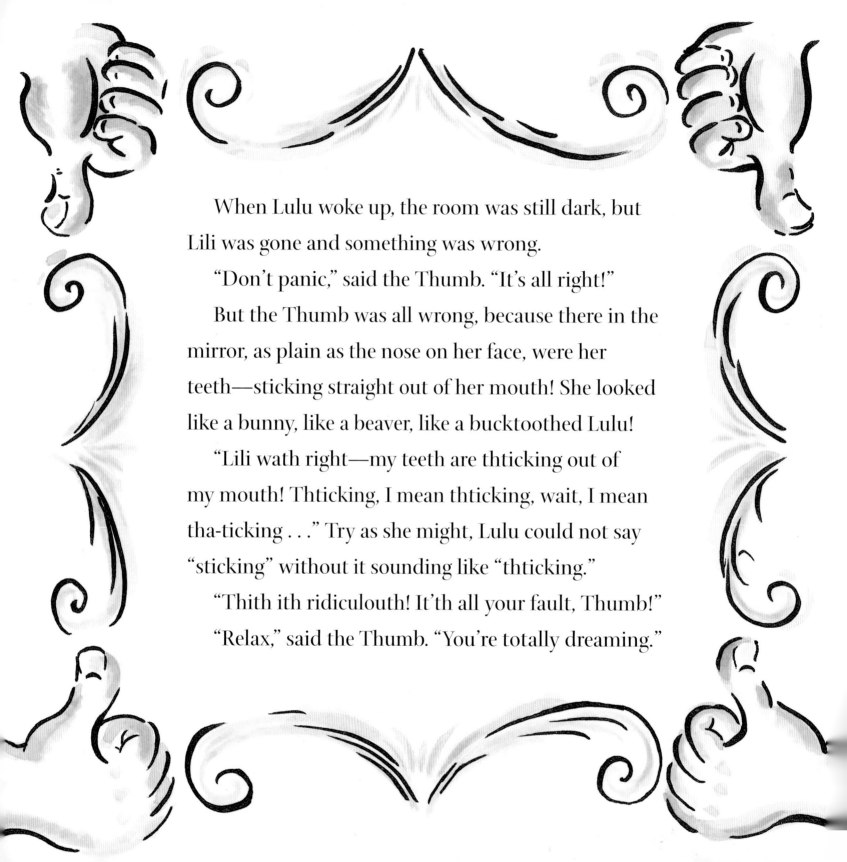

When Lulu woke up, the room was still dark, but Lili was gone and something was wrong.

"Don't panic," said the Thumb. "It's all right!"

But the Thumb was all wrong, because there in the mirror, as plain as the nose on her face, were her teeth—sticking straight out of her mouth! She looked like a bunny, like a beaver, like a bucktoothed Lulu!

"Lili wath right—my teeth are thticking out of my mouth! Thticking, I mean thticking, wait, I mean tha-ticking . . ." Try as she might, Lulu could not say "sticking" without it sounding like "thticking."

"Thith ith ridiculouth! It'th all your fault, Thumb!"

"Relax," said the Thumb. "You're totally dreaming."

Lulu woke up from her nightmare and heaved a sigh of relief.

"Thank goodness," she said—and repeated it just to make sure. "Thank goodness*ssss*!"

But that bad dream made Lulu see her Thumb in a different way.

"From now on we're not going to see so much of each other."

"NO!" said the Thumb.

"Yes," said Lulu. "Furthermore, I'm going to invent a program!"

"What kind of a program?" asked the Thumb.

"A program with steps!" Lulu shouted triumphantly.

And so it was that Lulu made up her mind to quit being a sucker.

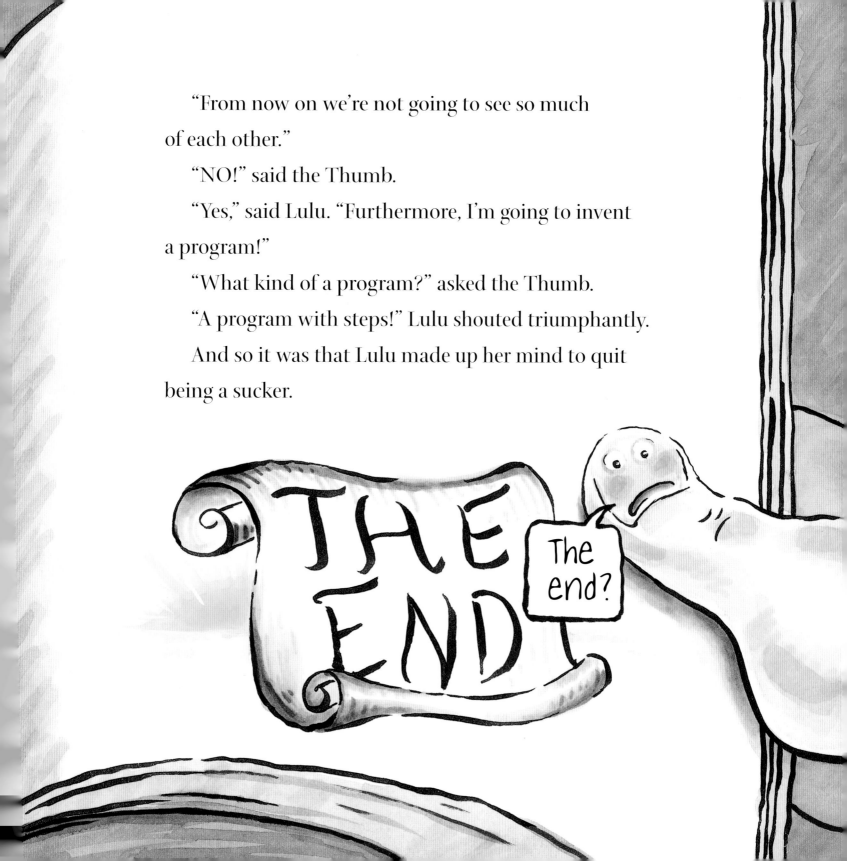

THE END

The end?

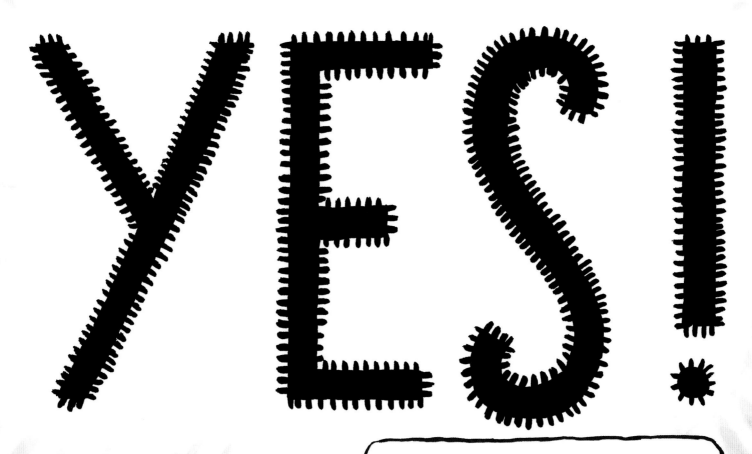

Step 1: Announce to friends and family that you have decided once and for all to quit sucking your thumb!

Lulu told everyone that she was kicking the habit. Everyone was incredibly impressed with her determination and resolve.

Step 2: Decide that you will only suck your thumb when nobody is looking.

But it turned out that quitting was not as easy as Lulu thought it would be.

Step 3: Realize that you will never be able to attend a slumber party, camp, or college if you continue to follow Step 2.

Step 4: Get a sock and put it over the Thumb you are trying to stop sucking.

HEY!!
LET ME OUT OF HERE!
COUGH, COUGH...
I CAN'T BREATHE...
CALL 911!

And while it was true that years of having its own way made that Thumb difficult to ignore sometimes . . .

Step 5: Before going to bed, dip the Thumb from Step 4 in Tabasco sauce.

. . . Lulu was determined to quit being a thumb sucker—even though she failed often and even though many times it was very painful for her.

Step 6: Repeat Steps 4 and 5. Before going to sleep, wedge arm attached to Thumb from Steps 4 and 5 under body. Do not remove till morning.

But Lulu was not going to let that Thumb get the better of her!

Step 7: Cover the offending Thumb with Play-Doh. Firmly pat into place and repeat Steps 4 through 6.

Step 8: Pick a date by which you want to stop sucking your thumb.

No matter how long it took . . .

Step 9: Pick another date.

. . . Lulu would never give up, because what she was gaining was far more important!

Step 10: Suggest to your parents that they reward you with money, toys, pets, and lavish vacations if you quit.

Step 11: If you fail . . .

. . . try again!

Sure, Lulu was losing the love of her Thumb . . .

. . . but nobody would EVER call her a baby again,
her teeth were right where they were supposed to be,
and she would be able to say "She sells seashells
by the seashore" as well as anyone.

Step 12: Carry the Message!

But most of all, Lulu had gained the skills she needed to help others stop sucking their thumbs . . .

WE LOVE YOU, LULU!

. . . and because of this, Lulu found some love.